The Jungle of Truth

Seamus Tracy and Marge Brown

Seamus
Tracy
enjoy the
book! ☺

Published by Quantum Results Publishing

November 2017

ISBN: 1977863671
ISBN-13:978-1977863676

Seamus Tracy and Marge Brown

DEDICATION

This book is dedicated to Cynthia Kersey,
President of The Unstoppable Foundation.

CONTENTS

ACKNOWLEDGMENTS

*The authors wish to acknowledge
Pete Brown for his cover design,
Bruce Brown and Rich Brown
for their executive editing advice, and
Liz Brown Tracy for her editing and support.*

PART ONE

STRONG

1

THE LIFE OF AN IMPOSTER

On this typical June day, I know the midday sun will create unbearable heat in the heart of the city. It might even hit 100 degrees at its peak. Nevertheless, I brace myself for another 12-hour working day along with hundreds of other policemen and police-women and detectives who toil to control crime in the sprawling capital.

Cairo, the City of a Thousand Minarets, is a majestic site with its preponderance of Islamic architecture. I enjoy starting my workdays with the sunrise about 5:00 a.m., as a detective in the Cairo Police Department.

My favorite part of each day is my workout time at Hers Gym. It's considered a high-end establishment. It's pricey for a single woman with a low-end salary like me, but my fitness is a priority.

After I hit 30 last year, I'm even more aware of the need to work hard on my strength and endurance, especially in my line of work. I also like the fact that it's a women's only gym, so I don't have to endure banter with aggressively flirtatious males.

I quickly dress in my workout clothes, pack my uniform, feed Azizi, my cat, and lock my apartment door on the way out. My car is nondescript but serviceable for navigating the congested Cairo traffic. Luckily the insanity won't start for a few hours, so I reach Hers in just a few minutes.

As usual, Rana is at the check-in desk, and she looks half asleep.

"Good morning, Detective Strong! You're

always more bright-eyed at this hour of the morning than our other members. I don't know how you do it! I can barely get out of bed to report to work on time. I have too much to do at home. You're lucky to be single."

"Well, Rana, you ought to take advantage of your job perks, and schedule a work out for yourself sometime soon."

"Yeah, you're right. I'll give that some serious thought. Here are your towel and key. Enjoy your workout!"

I go right to the abs machine. I purposely don't make eye contact with anyone else in the gym and only speak if it's necessary to be polite. This morning's session is how I prefer to spend my fitness hour – no conversation, open machines, and the opportunity to focus on improving my strength and endurance.

In the past, I hired one of the gym's

trainers, Heba, but canceled her contract soon after she signaled that she wanted to develop a friendship and make social plans with me. I like being a loner; I'm going to keep it that way. I notice Heba pacing around the gym this morning, and despite wanting to avoid her, I address her, so I don't appear too unfriendly.

"So, Heba, how's business?"

"Could be better, Amanda. A lot of my clients want to work with me in the afternoon, but not many want to schedule private sessions with me at dawn. I see you're staying committed to your fitness regimen."

"Yes, this is the only time of day when I can clear my head, work my muscles, and get ready for a long day of law enforcement. The tourist traffic is increasing each day. I have to be in the best shape possible."

"I hear you. I know you're happier working

out on your own, but if you ever decide to work with a trainer again, I'm at your service. And if you want to meet my friends and me for drinks some day after work, just send me a text, and I'll give you directions. They'd love to meet you!"

"Thanks, Heba. I barely have the energy to show up for my cat after work, so don't expect to hear from me anytime soon."

"No worries."

It feels good to sweat during my strenuous workout. Exercise keeps my mind straight and my emotions in check, two critical traits for a sharp detective like me.

I moved up the learning curve faster than most new detectives when I joined the force five years ago. As an English expat, I had stiff competition from the native Egyptians applying to the police force at the time. I nailed the fitness and psychological qualification tests, so the police board accepted my application with no questions asked.

During the grueling six months of training, the instructors and fellow trainees wanted to see me fail, but I wouldn't give them the satisfaction. I didn't make any friends, but I earned their grudging respect when I graduated at the top of my class.

My goal was to promote to Detective in two years. I received the promotion in a year and a half after solving a particularly nasty murder case that stumped my superiors for months. I know how to think like a criminal. My life depends on it.

Today, after a long and refreshing shower, I proudly don my distinguished navy-blue police uniform, adjust my Bluetooth headset, tie my white headscarf over my tangled blond hair, secure the scarf under my chin, adjust my white cap, and clasp my gold watch on my tanned wrist. I complete my official look with expensive sunglasses.

I'm ready for a long, hot day on the job. I believe neither my friends nor family members would recognize me in full uniform, and, more importantly, neither would Interpol detectives.

I requested to be assigned to patrol the Khan Al-Khalili bazaar, a popular and very crowded tourist destination across the road from the historic Al-Ashar Mosque. While there are lower ranking members of the police force also patrolling the bazaar, the Captain was happy to meet my request. He wants his most alert and agile detective to make her presence known in the open-air market.

This area of Cairo has been plagued with robberies lately. The shopkeepers are clamoring for extra police protection. The sight of me on daily patrols reassures them that they have additional protection against crafty street robbers and thieves like that Finn kid. I seriously hate him. He's cost my reputation a lot in the last few months.

I usually start my day in the bazaar with a cup of mint tea at El Fishawy Coffee Shop, one of the most famous cafes in the Arab world. I like the noise and smells of El Fishawy, with its wobbly and small brass-topped tables and charming waiters. A mix of locals and tourists gather there day and night to drink tea, coffee, and sahlab and smoke hookah pipes.

Today I claim a spot at my favorite corner table. My regular early-morning waiter, Ahmed, greets me on this bright summer day.

"Detective, will it be the usual this morning?"

"Yes, thanks, Ahmed. And how are you today?

"I'm happier now that you're here," he flirted with a big sincere smile.

As I wait for my order, I watch the pedestrian throngs start to build in the labyrinthine neighborhood, even at this early hour. Eventually, Ahmed works his way through the crowded café and appears with my mint tea. It is consistently flavorful, and I don't want to start my day without it.

"Are you studying hard, Ahmed?" I ask.

"Hard enough to get my degree next year."

"Stay focused. Don't let anyone or anything take you off track. Promise?"

Ahmed gives me a reassuring look. "You know I have big dreams. I won't be waiting tables here much longer. I plan to start my own business, make a lot of money, and marry my girlfriend, Farah."

"Take it from me. It's easy to get off track. I'll keep pestering you until I see that degree."

"Ok, it's a deal," agreed Ahmed.

As much as I enjoy my tea break and friendly banter with Ahmed, it's time for me to get moving in and around the Khan Al-Khalili bazaar.

The busy shopkeepers like me because I have a good reputation for catching pickpockets who prey on tourists. That is except the elusive Finn. I'll arrest him soon!

The visitors are often distracted by the crowds in the alleys, the confounding vehicle and pedestrian traffic in the surrounding streets, and the general stress of having to bargain with vendors for every item they want to buy. I wonder if they had a clue that for every sale, there is one price for tourists and a much lower price for Egyptians.

Sometimes the Sufi Dervishes perform their whirling dances to entertain and mesmerize the tourists. That's usually a time when the pickpockets are out in force.

The shadowy beggars and prowling vendors on every inch of cobblestone make it challenging for me to be a top-notch watchdog day in and day out in the teeming throng of humanity in the Khan Al-Khalili bazaar.

Luckily for me, it's a relatively quiet morning in the marketplace today. At about 11:30 a.m., I head to my favorite lunch spot, the Naguib Mahfouz Café, a refreshing indoor restaurant where I can temporarily escape my chaotic beat and grab my favorite sandwich, grilled pigeon.

I'm glad I don't know anyone at the café. I need a respite from the crowds and the rising heat outside. Just as I am finishing my last bite of my sandwich, another patron stops at my table and interrupts my precious solitude.

"Hello, Detective Strong. My name is Sherif. I own one of the most famous Egyptian sheet stalls in the Khan Al-Khalili. I want to give you a tip. There seems to be an upswing in young robbers who are trying to steal cash boxes from our stalls late in the day. It might be the work of a gang. I don't know. Please be on the lookout for these hooligans. If you can, position yourself near my shop towards the end of the day. I'd appreciate your help."

I look up from my nearly empty plate.

"Thanks for the tip, Sherif. You don't have to ask twice."

I'm especially alert at the end of the day when most of the vendors' cash boxes are full. This tip just reinforces my obsession to be known and respected as one of the most effective law enforcement officials to combat street crime in Cairo.

Despite Sherif's tip, there is no robbery or gang to pursue today. My day in the steamy bazaar comes to an end at 4:00 p.m.

I escape the hubbub and answer the late afternoon call for prayer at the Al-Azhar Mosque, which is across the street from the bazaar. This move is just another of my calculated attempts to blend in with the locals.

After feigning my respects at the mosque, I return home to my small apartment. Azizi, my black and white cat, greets me at the door. It's good to be responsible for one other living creature, but that's my limit.

Azizi requires little maintenance. Sometimes she scratches the furniture or escapes from the apartment. Usually, she's content being by herself, just like her owner.

I flip through my mail and find nothing unusual -- just the everyday bills and flyers. What I would give to have a letter from home! If my family and friends could reach me, then Interpol detectives would be fast to follow the trail. Connecting with the only people in the world who love me is out of the question.

With Azizi purring at my ankles, I heat leftover lamb and rice in the oven and sit down to eat with BBC Radio playing on my computer. Azizi settles down, satisfied that our quiet evening routine won't be disturbed.

Occasionally, I've played cards with my neighbors. I've been avoiding them lately, however, because they are always dropping hints that I need a husband, so I can break out of my solitary lifestyle. In my heart, I agree with them, but I'm resolved to hide my identity to avoid capture.

My middle-aged neighbor, Menna, is especially nosy about my lifestyle. She even offered to introduce me to her bachelor brother-in-law.

When I crossed paths with her in the apartment lobby last week, Menna asked, "Amanda, do you have any plans for the weekend?"

I answered, "Yes, I'm going away for the weekend to visit friends."

"Too bad," pouted Menna, "We're having a birthday party for my brother-in-law. I was hoping you could attend to meet some of my family members."

"Thanks, maybe next time," I said with relief.

I escaped to my apartment as fast as I could without being discourteous to Menna.

I'm adept at faking my preference for my solitary life. Menna's invitation last week only reinforced my deep nostalgia for my early years in Portsmouth, England. Secretly, I'm heartsick for my family and friends, and I avoid situations that make me feel vulnerable.

I especially miss my dad and the many hours we enjoyed together on his deep-sea fishing charter boat. He taught me power boating skills, so I could captain my charter fishing groups on his ship.

My navigation skills came in handy when I solved that open murder case. I used the Cairo police boat to chase the murderer down the River Nile for a dramatic capture that solidified my stellar reputation on the police force.

Those carefree days in England are a distant memory and thousands of miles away from my present-day life in Cairo. If only I had listened to my father when he cautioned me about the loser boyfriend I now wish I had never met!

My parents warned me about him. Characteristically and unfortunately, I didn't listen to them. Step by step the bum enticed me to join him five years ago in the artifact and art theft from the Campbells, a well-known archeologist couple in London.

Life is full of questions without answers. This big question has nagged me since the heist -- how the hell did I get pulled into his criminal web? It was too late to find the answer. I've paid the price since then by having to live incognito and always on guard.

I like my job. I can blend into the throngs of Cairo. I purposely keep a low profile. Unbeknownst to my superiors, I participated in the Campbell heist, thanks to my good-for-nothing, lame, idiotic, bad-news, ex-boyfriend, Sean.

So far, the police haven't caught us, but the case is still an Interpol priority. We're all laying low in various cities until we decide it's safe to move the goods and split the proceeds. Sean is in New York, Sarah's in El Salvador, Mike's in Hong Kong, and I'm here in Cairo. Raphael lost his life in the heist. I don't know how long I'll stay on the police force. For now, it's a perfect place to hide from the law -- in plain sight!

SARGE

2

A SOLDIER OF FORTUNE

"Sun's kind of hot today." I think to myself. Then again, it is high noon.

I just got up. I rock in my beat-up chair on the roof lounge, sipping my morning coffee. My roof wasn't built to be a place for anything but a prayer area. I'm Catholic and don't pray five times a day as the Muslims do. So, instead of using a prayer rug, I dragged some furniture up to the roof and called it my living room.

I have a small house, which is unusual in this neighborhood. When I was looking for a place to settle in Cairo, an old, rotted out apartment building collapsed. The owner didn't have the money to rebuild. He was willing to sell the lot to me for a cheap price seeing as I grew up in Cairo. Egyptians usually don't like doing business with expats and tourists.

I hired a crew to build a tiny one-bedroom house, and they managed to construct it in a month. They made this prayer roof assuming I was Muslim. I'm not surprised, because I look like an Egyptian, although I feel like an expat after my decades of service in the British Navy.

I have a clear view of the bazaar. Sometimes I eavesdrop on the stall right next to me in the alley. It's amusing to listen to the flabbergasted tourists that are so stressed out from bargaining with the cunning vendors.

Right below, there's an Egyptian kid negotiating prices on some sheets. Sherif's tough, though. He's not giving in at all.

"What the?"

The kid just stole a washcloth! But Sherif

doesn't have a clue! The kid snagged it like an expert!

I don't like to interfere, but I think I'll report him to the police. Sherif could and would try to sue me for witnessing the theft and not saying anything. Not that he would know that I didn't report the robbery, but I can't stomach the injustice.

Plus, Detective Strong would give me a pretty penny for a proven tip. I know her vaguely from around the alleys. She often stations herself at the bazaar, so she can grab some tea. She's given me cash for tips plenty of times.

I see her right now. She's talking to that waiter guy, Ahmed. No wonder she missed that brazen kid.

I get up and walk over to the balcony to get a better look at this kid. He looks about fourteen with shaggy, unkempt, light brown hair. It hangs to his shoulders, and the edges are rough like he cuts it with a knife.

He's undoubtedly homeless. His clothes are torn and ragged from being worn so much. I think he's wearing the remnants of a red sweatshirt, green sneakers, and blue jeans. But honestly, it's hard to make them out on his thin frame.

His sneakers are the only thing remotely new. I'll bet he stole them from a stall or took money to buy them recently. I wonder where he calls home.

Then a second street kid, who looks a few years older than the first kid and who's wearing the same style of green sneakers, walks by the stall.

Sherif notices him, too, "That your brother?" he asks the first kid.

"Oh, him?" The older boy starts to answer.

" Well ... uh, he's" -- but he doesn't get to finish.

Suddenly, the older boy snatches a wallet from the hip pocket of an American tourist.

They're always loaded with cash.

Sherif, who appears to be the only one who notices, runs and tries to catch the kid.

The kid jumps through a tiny first-floor window of a hotel. Unfortunately, Sherif can't fit through the window.

By now the kid's long gone, anyway.

Sherif finds Detective Strong to tell her about what happened. I overhear their conversation from my perch.

"Detective, I've had it with these street thieves! When is the Cairo police force going to do something about this threat to the bazaar vendors?"

"We're on it, Sherif!" shouted Strong, as she blew her piercing police whistle.

I turn my attention back to the younger kid. But he's not there. Then I spot him running away from the stall.

"I wonder why he's going back to the alley," I say aloud.

He just sprinted past the stall, so I decide to follow him. I could get a decent payoff for reporting where he sleeps. I might even get a permanent discount from Sherif!

I dash downstairs and slip out the front door. The kid is much more cautious now. He's crouched down. I duck below a stack of crates, so he can't see me.

I was right; he turns around to check for a tail. He doesn't see me. Then he slips into a door that I didn't even notice before! It blends right in with the building's south wall.

A few minutes later, I follow him inside the nameless structure. I enter a dingy thirty-foot square room. I'm stunned to see all this kid owns is a twin mattress with one soiled sheet, undoubtedly stolen from Sherif.

But I don't have much time to look around.

The kid suddenly pops out of the shadows, right in front of me!

He can't be older than twelve or so, now that I see him up close. He's not old enough to be too suspicious. I wonder why he isn't rich. From what I've seen, he could do it with ease. He's a master thief!

Then it hits me! This kid's not stealing for the fun of it. He has no other option!

There's no way I'm going to report him now!

"Uh, hi, I'm" -- I stammer, but he cuts me off.

"I'm Finn, and I don't care!"

He uppercuts me into the steel door behind me. Then everything goes black.

I wake up, leaning against the cold steel, with a throbbing headache. With exhaustive effort, I manage to retrace my steps to my front door. I stumble into the kitchen and take a few aspirin.

Judging by the sun, it's very early in the morning – almost a whole day from when that kid hit me!

There's no one on the streets. I stagger down the alley to the door and fling it open. The kid's gone! He just got up and left!

Back at my small house, I nurse my aching head on the rooftop. As the sun starts to rise higher in the sky, I overhear Strong talking to Ahmed again.

"Hey, Ahmed, I don't know about you, but I'm feeling stressed lately. I need a day on the water to relax. I'm going to the Suez Yacht Club early tomorrow morning to take my boat out. There's nothing like a few hours on the *Quest* to unwind."

Ahmed sighed. "I'll think of you while I'm waiting tables in the sweltering sun! And, I'll keep my eye out for those street thieves!"

"Thanks, Ahmed! I'll make it worth it to you if you do. I want those juvenile delinquents behind bars!"

FINN

3

THE DREAM

"How the hell did he find me?" I wonder as I race through Cairo's complicated alleyway grid.

I've memorized the network by now. Today isn't the first time I've needed to make a quick escape. I thought I had checked behind me, but I guess I was careless. I need to be more watchful.

I've been super careful in my years of thievery. I move every time I get a sideways look or something like the close call I had with the guy in the alley. Truthfully, I'm lucky I knocked him out. It was due much more to the weight of the steel door hitting his head than to my strength.

I only have a few possessions, including the clothes on my back and a schoolboy's backpack to conceal stolen items.

"I need a place to hide. I need a place to hide. I need a place to hide!" I repeat to myself.

Then I see a big crowd off to my right. Perfect, I can put on my schoolboy act again!

I turn and sprint into the throng. When I get to the front of the crowd, I see what the people are watching -- a traveling circus! Currently, there's an Asian man throwing cards and using them to slice into watermelons and apples. He has an unusual talent that is mesmerizing to watch.

Hey, why not hide and have fun at the same time? As I gaze at the acrobats making a human pyramid, I realize something. Those cards could be used to cut flesh instead of fruit! I slip through the onlookers and get behind the performers' trailer. I wait a few minutes until every performer is on stage collecting tips and signing autographs. I decide to make my move.

I pull out a lock pick from my backpack and break the trailer door's steel padlock. It falls away, but I catch it before it clangs on the rocky ground. I slip it in my pocket and slide myself through the door.

I find myself in a large room full of supplies. I search until I find a stack of card decks in a locker, which must belong to the Asian dude. I nab a few and try to copy his movements. My card flutters about two feet around my head like a butterfly and then falls to the ground.

At first, I'm disappointed, but then I remember that no one gets anything right the first time. I also see a paper with notes and tips about card throwing. I steal it as well.

Suddenly, I hear footsteps and chatter. The performers are coming back! I hop into a small locker and quietly shut the door behind me.

Just in time!

I hear shouts through the partially opened door. Suddenly the door bangs open! They barge in and begin to look around. Honestly, the way they tore the place apart, they probably cost themselves more money than I ever would have.

An ape-looking man, so large his muscles have muscles, comes so close to my hiding place that I can hear him breathing. He smells horrible! I beat down my gag reflex.

Finally, they decide I must have slipped away, and they run out the door after 'me'.

I wait for at least ten minutes, catching my breath. I finally escape figuring it's only a matter of time before the ape-man comes back and dents my head in for his next trick. The cops would give a sack of Egyptian pounds to see that one. I chuckle at my fantasy then head off to find shelter.

After I run a block or two, I slip around a corner into an old hiding place of mine. I found it a couple of years back running from Detective Strong. She's one of the cops that seriously wants my blood, probably the most of all of them. I can't blame her! I almost got her kicked off the force! Three times!

I sit down in the shadow of a dumpster hidden away from the busy road. I plot my next move. I can't stay here. Strong always patrols my past hiding places hoping to catch me.

I'll get some sleep and then get moving before 7:30 a.m. That's when the detective patrols. I only know this since I once followed her to learn her habits, so I could stay out of her way. She came by the day after at the same exact time. She is a professional with a predictable schedule.

But for now, I lie down in the alley's shadows and sleep. When I wake up the sun isn't very high. It must be around 7:20 a.m. Oh crap!

"Hello, Finn." The voice cuts through the air like a knife, sharp and cold. I'd recognize it anywhere.

"Detective Strong?" I blurt out.

"Yes, It's me! You're done, Finn."

She spits out my name like it tasted horrible.

4

A TYPICAL DAY IN THE BAZAAR – NOT!

I shoot out of my bed from a deep sleep.

"Crap! Crap! Crap! Crap! Crap!" I scream.

It takes me about thirty seconds to realize I had a scary dream, but a veiled message too. I should get moving.

I try to awake. I'm not a morning person. As I get up, I can feel the heat, which could be any day in Cairo.

I didn't plan to sleep so late.

I stand up, rub my eyes, and pick up my bag from where I left it earlier. I wonder what I'll do now. I could try to nick some food.

My stomach is roaring at me like a lion in a fight with a gladiator. I read some stuff about Ancient Rome in a book that I stole from a library that described such a combat.

By the way, any library is a jackpot for homeless people - - you can be safe, warm, and entertained, at least until they kick you out. I had managed to avoid that last bit by toting a backpack to pretend I was studying for a school report.

I decide to give in to my roaring stomach and head to the marketplace.

I stroll past the stalls, acting innocent. As I pass a fruit cart, I move my hand to test the thickness of a melon, and as I do my dragging sleeve brushes the neatly stacked Red Delicious apples. Two apples fall inside my shirt! I gracefully move, so they tumble out of the bottom of my shirt. Each apple conveniently lands in my pants pockets, one on the left and one on the right.

Then I walk down the vendor rows until I get to another Red Delicious apple section. I silently slip my backpack off and unzip the back pocket. I perform the same trick, pretending to look at bananas. Three more Red Delicious apples fall into my backpack.

I pick up the pack up by its worn strap and walk hunched over like the bag was hurting my back. I can't let any of my movements look random or suspicious.

Suddenly, I see a one-pound bill on the ground! I quickly grab it.

I turn to a vendor. "One melon please."

"Uh, that's a 100-pound note," he stammers.

"Keep the change," I tell him.

Okay, yes, I felt a little guilty.

When he opens the register, I see a massive stack of 100-pound notes!

The vendor glances up, "Hey, kid. I need to use the bathroom will you watch the stall?"

My innocent act worked!

As soon as the vendor moves out of sight, I snag the huge stack of notes. I scurry down the closest alley without looking back.

Suddenly I see the familiar blue of a police uniform. I run for it, zooming in and out of the maze of narrow alleys. Then another cop pops out of a lane in a patrol car and lands the car right in front of me. As it shimmies to a stop, the rubber tires make a high-pitched squeal on the pavement.

The police car's front passenger door is around five yards away from me. The cop in the car jumps out the other side. He looks like a rookie - - his uniform fits loosely, sweat is pouring off his brow, his taser is shaking in his hand. He seems very hesitant to use it.

"Wait, taser!?! Crap!"

I jump closer to the car's passenger door, and the cop starts to run around the hood of the car. With seconds to spare I catapult myself over the hood of the car. I feel my right foot connect with something and hear a scream of pain. The taser clatters to the pavement, and I scoop it up. I turn to face the dude. He's staggering away with blood dripping from a broken nose.

I decide that he won't give me trouble for a second and look around for the other cop, who is standing right behind me! This one's female. I thought it was Strong for a second and panicked, but it was just my paranoia. I have no idea who this cop is. I decide to stop caring who she is and just blast her with the taser. So, I do. Her short blond hair stands on end, and she face-plants right in front of my shoe.

I try the same move on the foot patrol cop who suddenly appears from an adjacent alley, but my tactic doesn't work. The taser needs to recharge! He lunges to attack me with his baton. I throw the taser aside and kick him firmly in the crotch as he attempts to swing his weapon. His eyes go wide, and he falls to the ground. This cop lands on his side in a fetal position. He says something to me, but I can't hear a sound, though I can read his lips.

I throw open the door of the cop car and jump in behind the steering wheel. The engine is still running. I floor it and jerk the wheel to the left. Too late! The back of the car slams into a building and careens for about twenty feet before spinning and ramming into a stall. It scatters fresh produce along the road. The car turns and drifts out of the minefield of slippery fruit guts facing backward.

I do a tight U-turn by jerking the wheel. This maneuver causes the patrol car to fishtail for a few seconds. About 90% of my mind says this is a horrible idea, and I should get out and run on foot, but I do not listen to myself, so I keep going.

I decide that if I ever manage to take my driver's test in five years, I would never pass. Ever.

I speed down the streets at eighty miles an hour taking random turns whenever I hit a crossroads. Unfortunately, I have pursuers -- three cop cars.

We come to a four-way intersection, and I hear the car radio beep.

A voice comes on the radio, "Omar, Youssef, and Ayman, turn and flank him up ahead. Run your cars into him when you catch him, but you guys bail out before you hit him. Get your speed up to around 120, so you can be there when he arrives."

"The fools! They forgot to switch channels, so I can hear everything they plan."

I keep driving at high speed. I have a plan. Sure enough a few minutes later I come to another intersection. I see the three cop cars but force myself to keep going. When the vehicles accelerate in my direction, I slam on the brakes and put my car in reverse. When the collision happens, I am not a part of it, and neither are the cops, who jump to the pavement as ordered.

The three police cars hit each other at full

speed and immediately go up in flames. The cars' hoods squish just like a soft hamburger bun in the tight grip of an enthusiastic rock band fan. I see the police troopers run away from me, towards the Egyptian Museum in Tahrir Square.

"Wait! That's it! The museum is the perfect hiding place! I can lose anyone in there!" I shout with glee.

I know the museum inside out. My Aunt Linda took me there many times when I was little. She was a would-be historian. My parents were always away on their archaeologist missions.

My most explicit memory of Aunt Linda is her reading my *Curious George Goes Camping* book to me while I tried to sleep in my crib.

Eventually, my aunt went to a retirement home, and the authorities sent me to an orphanage.

When I was ten years old, I broke out of the

orphanage and found myself living on the streets with no idea how to find my parents or get to our home in New York.

I might make it through this day after all.

Suddenly the radio voice comes back on.

"Sounds good, Finn. See you there."

The radio beeps some more. It's the lead officer again, and this time I know who is behind the wheel of that suspicious car behind me - - Detective Amanda Strong.

"Oh no! They can hear me, too! "

This situation is bad. The last time we met Strong gave me a bloody nose, black eye, and swollen lip.

I slam the car into drive and do a tight U-turn again. I whiz right past Strong's car. Our side mirrors collide, and glass particles spray in every direction. As I pass her, I see her stunned look. She can't react fast enough to catch me.

This time I floor it. I shoot down the alleyways and find the spot where the cops tried to jump me. At last, I see the road to the museum. I take a sharp turn onto the two-way road. I speed down it until I locate the barricade in front of the museum. Instead of turning, I keep going straight.

"If I keep going, I can rush through the doors of the main entrance... right here!" I declare.

I jump out of the car and sprint to the main entrance doors of the museum. Fortunately, it's already Sunday evening, so it'll be empty. I pull at the door handles with no luck.

"Oh no. I'm locked out!"

I should've predicted this! And now Strong will be here to arrest me in a few minutes!

5

A MYSTERY UNFOLDS

"Strong is not going to take me this time!" I exclaim.

I hear her siren – she's closing in fast.

"I have to break the lock!"

I remember the stolen stash of cards in my backpack. If they can slice a melon, then maybe they can slice through this lock. My hands are trembling like crazy.

"Hurry! Hurry!" I whisper to myself.

My voice is shaking as much as my hands now.

"Yes! It worked! I'm in!"

Relief sets in like a dense fog.

Detective Strong's battered car rumbles to a stop at the front door of the Egyptian Museum. She jumps out and runs up the front steps two at a time, tearing off her sunglasses as she sprints.

"Thank God, it's closed for the day. Finn is mine now!"

As Strong enters the museum, she radios headquarters through her Bluetooth headset.

"Calling for backup. Send another squad to the Egyptian Museum to circle the building. I want a tight net, so there's no chance for Finn to escape. We've got him this time!"

Strong mentally reviews the list of offenses she can pin on the 12-year-old delinquent: stealing goods, leaving the scene of a crime, assaulting an officer, hijacking a police car, driving without a license, destroying public property, breaking and entering, endangering the lives of pedestrians, speeding, driving recklessly, damaging private property, and failing to obey a police officer. And that's just a start. By the time she's finished with him, he'll be aging like a good cigar in a hot Egyptian prison cell.

Even though the Egyptian Museum has over 100 halls of exhibit space spread over two floors, Strong is confident she can nab her prey.

She's obsessed with catching the slippery Finn, and now she can book him with a list of offenses beyond her wildest dreams.

Where to start looking? She decides to cover the museum floors very methodically with a cool head.

Finn could be hiding in any of the hundreds of exhibits displaying over 160,000 objects from Egypt's previous 5,000 years. There's also a cafeteria, bank, post office, gift shop, library, and children's museum to compound matters.

With flashlight in hand, Strong grabs a map of the museum's floor plan and begins her careful search.

Quickly and quietly circling the main halls of the entire first floor, Strong sees no sign of Finn.

She decides that it's likely he escaped to the second floor to hide among the mummies. That's what she would do if she were in his stolen shoes!

Her squad is still untangling their burning cars from the pileup. There's no sign of the new team yet.

Finn cowers behind an ancient mummy display in one of the side hallways in the museum's second floor. He hears Strong fly up the stairs in determined pursuit. The only way out for Finn now is to escape in the nearby elevator.

"What? Crap!"

An elevator sign says you must ask the trained engineer to operate it. Finn quickly loots the mechanic's office next to the elevator and finds the operating instructions.

Finn starts to panic as he hears Strong's footsteps rapidly approaching the elevator area.

Just as Strong turns the corner and spots the elevator, Finn gets it to operate. He quickly opens and closes the doors and hits the button for the basement. He bought some valuable time.

Detective Strong sees the elevator button light up for the basement level. Now she's sure Finn is taking his last ride. She contacts her new squad members, who just arrived at the museum's entrance.

"The perpetrator is headed for the basement. Copy."

"The building's surrounded. We've got our kid this time, Detective Strong. Officers Forbes and Kawamura will meet you in the basement for his arrest."

"Your days of freedom are over now, Finn."

Strong can't hide her excitement as she bounds down two flights of stairs to corner Finn in the museum basement.

"There's no way out for you," she hisses.

The museum's basement is dense with scaffolding and dust. A subterranean renovation is underway. Finn starts to sneeze from all the pollutants in the air. He looks down and realizes he's leaving footprints in the dust. Between his sneezing and his prints, he might as well put a target on his back to make it easy for Detective Strong and her officers to throw their net over him.

"Quick, I need an escape plan," Finn says aloud to himself.

The young fugitive looks up to say a quick prayer of desperation.

"Ah, I think I see my way out."

At the top of the basement walls, Finn spots a ground level window with an adjacent air duct. A plan pops into his wily mind.

In the dim light of the smelly and spooky basement, Strong connects with Forbes and Kawamura. Their flashlights illuminate the dusty footprints. They look at each other with knowing expressions. Suddenly, Finn's capture feels too easy.

They're suspicious and on their guard, but the team is ready to seize Finn by the scruff of his dirty neck. They have the building surrounded, so there's no way they can fail this time.

The dusty footprints lead to an open basement window. It looks like Finn found an easy exit.

"He can leave the building, but he can't outwit the Cairo police force this time," Strong tells her team.

She contacts the lead officer outside the quiet museum and tells him to position the team on the east building wall with the open window. They should have Finn in the back of a police car within a few minutes.

Strong is so confident of Finn's capture that she instructs her officers to walk with her back up to the museum's first floor and out through the front door rather than pursue Finn through the open basement window.

She and her team approach the squad cars, which are ablaze with flashing lights.

She asks the nearest cop, "So which car is holding Finn?"

The cop looks at her with a confused expression.

"We thought you were bringing him in. We

haven't seen any sign of him."

Strong throws her police cap on the ground and stomps on it. She drops and breaks her Bluetooth headset in the process.

"This is not possible!" she screams.

"I'm going to get that kid if I have to go to the ends of the earth."

With the sound of minarets announcing sunset prayers across Cairo, the beleaguered cops fan out into the crowded streets and narrow alleys to search for their elusive prey.

Meanwhile, inside the museum, Finn drops out of the ventilator tube, holding his sneakers close to his chest.

Finn speaks to the basement ghosts, "That was a close call. The closest call I've ever had with Strong. She'll be on my trail now. I better lay low in the museum tonight, and come up with a new plan for the rest of my life."

As the adrenaline drains from his system, Finn begins to feel hunger pains. Luckily, he finds the five pilfered Red Delicious apples in his backpack along with the wads of cash he stole from the marketplace. The apples will have to be dinner and breakfast.

There's no way he is going to make a break for it until dawn. He wants to time his getaway before the renovation work crews arrive and the museum opens.

Finn sits down on the dusty floor and eats two apples. That's enough to fill his stomach after one of the most exciting days of his life. He falls asleep on the basement floor with his backpack under his head and old carton flaps providing a bit of warmth under and over his spent body.

It must have been about 3:00 a.m. when Finn stirs, hearing the scurrying mice. He knows he'll get no more sleep that night. To calm his growling stomach, he takes another apple from his backpack and eats it slowly in the semi-darkness of the cavernous basement.

"There must be something here to take my mind off my plight for a few hours," Finn ponders.

Feeling alone and bored, Finn strategies aloud, "There are a lot of boxes on these dusty shelves. Maybe I can learn something about Egyptian history while I'm waiting to bust out of here in a few hours."

In the dim light, Finn starts walking up and down the aisles, running his dirty fingers across the labels on the old storage boxes. There are many archived records stored here. Most were related to subjects which are completely unfamiliar and of little interest to him. Why would he want to learn about the ancient jackal god called Wepwawet, the Hungarian excavations at Thebes, the statue of Ramessesnakht, or the Tomb of Maia at Saqqara?

Even though Finn is always looking for ways to develop his street smarts, he doubts these ancient archives would do much for his practical education.

Trying to stay awake, Finn absentmindedly runs his fingers over the labels on some old boxes. A handwritten tag about a "Lost Archeologist Couple" catches his attention.

"That sounds intriguing," mutters Finn, feeling more awake now.

With no small effort, he removes the heavy, large, beat-up box from the dusty shelf. He pulls the carton over to a spot on the floor where he uses a ray of moonlight to examine its contents.

At first glance, there wasn't much in the box of interest to Finn – just some old maps and letters. He feels something substantial at the bottom of the box and carefully pulls it out.

It's an engraved plaque. Finn struggles to read the inscription in the moonlight. It's a commendation to Alice and Tom Campbell, archeologists emeriti.

Apparently, these two historians, who originally hailed from New York, made substantial progress in excavating ruins in Madagascar 10 years ago.

"Wait, those two could be my parents!" exclaims Finn aloud.

Was this the missing piece of his history? Were his parents last seen in Madagascar?

With more digging, Finn uncovers several old newspaper articles in the box. They confirm his suspicions. His parents left him with his Aunt Linda when they went excavating, and she died before she could tell him about their fate.

Next, the boy uncovers a photo of Alice and Tom as a young couple with their newborn son, Finn.

"Finn! That's me! So, what happened to my parents? Why didn't they return from Madagascar?"

There's no time to ask more questions. Finn grabs all the evidence he could stuff in his backpack. His plan was clear.

Finn will travel to Madagascar to find out what happened to his parents. He'll work out the details once he gets moving.

As daylight breaks, any alert pedestrian crossing Tahrir Square could detect a young boy squirming out of a small basement window in the Egyptian Museum.

Across town, Detective Amanda Strong and her team set up an incident room to focus on capturing the elusive Finn. This was war!!

6

CALL TO ADVENTURE

I scuttle through a dirty, smelly, gross alleyway with only one goal-- find answers. Questions are zipping through my brain in and out of focus like a swarm of bees. The only way to satisfy my dilemma is to get answers, and fortunately, I know where to look.

After my Aunt Linda moved to the retirement home, an earthquake shook the Tahrir Square vicinity, including her abandoned home. She lived nearby the square on Meret Basha street near the Egyptian Night hotel. Her house was slightly damaged, and no one cared about it or fixed it up, so it's still there.

I screech to a stop about halfway there. People are waking up! I see lights flickering on in windows. Crap! All of Cairo knows my face and the citizens are eager to make some cash helping the police.

Strong put out a 'Fugitive Alert' on me. I heard her give the command when I was hiding in the vent at the museum. The small vent opened over her 'tantrum spot' outside the museum. I witnessed with glee while she threw an epic tantrum -- stomping, swearing, screaming, raging, and randomly punching the person closest to her! It was a grand display! I almost gave myself away laughing.

I jump up and grab a storm drain. The cops won't see me on top of the buildings. I pull myself up, inch by inch struggling for a grip on the morning dew covered pipe. I finally manage to reach the rooftop and pull myself over the edge. I just lay there for a minute contemplating what I should do when I get to my aunt's former house. Maybe I'll raid her hidden safe. I could get information about my parents from her computer, too.

I rise to my feet and start running. The distance to the drop off from the roof's edge narrows -- three yards, two, one. On my next landing, I only leave my foot on the roof for a nanosecond before I push off and land on the roof of another house. And then I do it again.

I hear footsteps. The city's faithful are starting to answer the call to morning prayers! Thinking quickly, I slide off the edge of the roof onto an air conditioner. I shoulder through the nearby window with a loud crash. The glass particles cut my skin, but I barely feel the gash.

I hear a shout from a man on a nearby roof. Soon he disappears, and I keep going.

Then I hear more shouts. The man is following me! As I glance back, I can't see what's in front of me in the dark room. Crash! I hit the floor hard.

I struggle to get up and soon realize I'm in

someone's home. As I turn to escape, the door abruptly swings open, and large hands cover my mouth and my unknown assailant shoves me back into the house and onto the floor.

I look up to identify my captor, but he slams me to the ground. My nose makes contact with the floor, and I see a puddle of red spreading toward my eye. The red fades to black, and I pass out.

I wake up and see nothing. I hear my ragged breath, but this barely registers in my mind before I pass out again.

The next time I'm awake I realize I'm in a bed. I see a strange man.

"Oh crap, he's going to kill me."

I know that this is illogical since he's trying to help me recover. I try to run. Try. I can't move! Then I burn out again like a broken lightbulb.

The next few times I try to get up and run

the same thing happens. Finally, after many attempts, I can move! I crawl out of bed and stand, but as soon as I do, I feel a shockwave of pain in my skull! I scream and collapse on the floor. This insanity continues. I don't try to get out of bed again.

I have no idea how long I've been here. My blackouts could have lasted a second or a week. Gradually I find that I can move a little more freely. I pick up my head -- no pain. I try sitting up, and I feel a small headache, but I ignore it. When I'm finally able to stand, the throbbing gets worse.

Apparently, I never made it to Aunt Linda's abandoned house. I stumble out of the unfamiliar room into the kitchen and find the mystery man sitting at the table. I smelled the coffee brewing a minute ago but thought the kitchen was downstairs! I feel dizzy and disoriented.

"Finn, why don't you tell me, in your own words, what happened? Oh, and by the way, you can call me Sarge," the man said.

So, I do. I tell Sarge everything about my life on the streets and my recent decision to go to Madagascar to uncover my parents' fate. I don't know why. I guess I just trust him because he came to my aid, so I could stop running. The rhythmic clock ticked as we share Egyptian coffee from his worn coffee pot. Once we finish, I see he is forming a critical thought.

"Give me your stolen cash, and I'll take you to Madagascar," he announced.

This offer shocked me. "What? Do you have a boat? And, why?!?"

"Well, I know what you're going through with your life on the streets. My childhood was a lot like yours. My father was a war journalist, and my mother was a teacher. They were British, but we lived in Cairo, so my father could get home often. I ran off and joined the British Navy as soon as they would take me. I served all over the world for over 30 years. I know the sea," explained Sarge.

Sarge continued. "And a boat? No, I don't have one. But Strong does! Up for a little revenge?"

"Umm...What?"

"Oh Finn," he sighs mockingly, "I thought that theft was what you do best!"

With that, he turns and leaves. I scurry after him wondering whether I should trust this grizzled military vet.

PART TWO

7

A FORGED PARTNERSHIP

Sarge decided to let Finn sleep it off because the boy needed more rest before they left for Madagascar. He wondered if Finn had any idea that they were going to be navigating thousands of miles through treacherous seas!

"I'll soft peddle the dangers to him - like stormy weather or mechanical troubles or even pirates," thought Sarge.

Sarge pulled his thoughts back to their priority. They needed a boat. Luckily Strong's cruiser would fit the bill. Earlier that morning, Sarge called the Suez Yacht Club and told them he was interested in buying Strong's boat, the *Quest*. He mentioned to the port captain that he didn't trust her to give him the right specs, so he asked him to provide a rundown on the craft.

Sarge promised the port captain a hefty baksheesh when he and Finn arrived the next day to take a test drive in the *Quest*. That seemed to work the magic he needed with the guy.

From the port captain, Sarge learned that the *Quest* was a 2008 38-feet triple outboard Fountain 38 LX with a top speed of 60 mph and a range of 300 miles. He figured at its cruising speed of 40 mph they could get 450 miles out of her 325-gallon tank.

"I'm not crazy enough to plan to make a lot of stops for gas on the Somalia coast, although the pirate activity is supposedly dying down," considered Sarge.

While Sarge weighed the pirate threat, Finn stumbled onto the rooftop, rubbing his battered face. His host handed him a cup of strong Egyptian coffee.

"We don't have much time to sleep, kid. It's time to get ready for our getaway. Here's the plan. Tomorrow morning we're going to take a bus to the Suez Yacht Club and steal Strong's boat. Perfect, right? Then we're going to cruise about 4400 miles to Madagascar. It's going to take us about two and a half weeks if all goes well. But, we can't count on that. There could be surprises along the way."

He handed Finn a single sheet with their route. Finn was barely awake, but he perked up when he read through the plan.

Navigation Plan

Suez, Egypt > Hurghada, Egypt ....**234 miles**

Hurghada, Egypt > Marsa Ala, Egypt ....**165 miles**

Marsa Alam, Egypt > Port Sudan, Sudan... **165 miles**

Port Sudan, Sudan > Massawa, Eritrea .... **313 miles**

Massawa, Eritrea > Djibouti, Djibouti ....**373 miles**

Djibouti, Djibouti > Xiis, Somalia – ....**300 miles**

Xiis, Somalia > Bereeda, Somalia – ....**289 miles**

Bereeda, Somalia > Eyl, Somalia – ....**282 miles**

Eyl, Somalia > Ceeldhere, Somalia ....**338 miles**

Ceeldere, Somalia > Mogadishu, Somalia **179 miles**

Mogadishu, Somalia > Kismayo, Somalia...**254 miles**

Kismayo, Somalia > Malindi, Kenya ....**260 miles**

Malindi, Kenya > Tanga, Tanzania ....**147 miles**

Tanga, Tanzania > Dar es Salaam,
Tanzania ....**255 miles**

Dar es Salaam, Tanzania > Mtwara,
Tanzania...**252 miles**

Mtwara, Tanzania > Bouenindi, Comoros **228 miles**

Bouendini, Comoros > Mtsamboro,

Mayotte ....**144 miles**

Mtsamboro, Mayotte > Anorotsangana,
Madagascar ....**209 miles**

Total – 4387 miles

"We need supplies to last us for three weeks at sea. I've made us a shopping list. I need some cash, so I can go shopping alone. We can't let anyone see your face in public."

Finn considered the logical request from Sarge. Was he going to trust this old navy vet with his stolen money and his life or go back to scrambling on the streets and outrunning Strong? After studying the navigation plan, he knew he couldn't make it to Madagascar on his own.

It was the moment of truth. Finn knew he had to find out what happened to his parents and why they never returned from Madagascar. He retrieved the cash and handed a wad to Sarge.

"This should cover our supplies. The sooner

we leave the better."

Sarge breathed a sigh of relief. Their bond was firm.

He grabbed the cash and prepared to leave, shouting behind him, "You call the Kiwi Taxi Company and reserve a taxi for early tomorrow morning. Have them pick us up here and take us directly to the Suez Yacht Club. We want a private taxi with no stops!"

That night Finn helped Sarge pack their supplies in a few duffle bags. They didn't have a lot to say to each other. They both had a lot to think about to prepare for the long trip ahead.

Sleep was elusive for the adventurers. At the crack of dawn, the city's wailing minarets called them out of their beds for more strong coffee and a final strategy session.

"Ok, kid, this is it. We leave today, and there's no turning back. Are you ready?"

Finn pulled his cap down over his face to avoid recognition, and he nodded.

The taxi pulled up right on time. With the help of the driver, they loaded their supply bags and settled in for the 77-mile drive to the Suez Yacht Club. They faked sleep to avoid conversation with the driver.

"Approaching the Suez Yacht Club," hollered the driver, trying to awake his passengers.

As they disembarked, the cab driver tried to be helpful with their supply bags. In the process of hefting the oversize duffle bag out of the trunk, he swung it over his shoulder and knocked Finn's hat off his head. Finn scrambled to pick it up and put it on again to maintain his disguise. To his dismay, the driver got a good look at his face. They gazed at each other with startled expressions.

Sarge noticed the debacle and pulled out a wad of cash to appease the driver with more than the expected baksheesh.

"I hope this encourages you to forget this fare."

The driver nodded his assent that he wouldn't report them, but Sarge wasn't convinced.

Sarge turned to Finn, "We must keep moving fast. Strong won't be far behind after this careless mistake."

8

A RACE AT SEA

Detective Strong spent time each morning in her incident room rethinking her strategy for capturing Finn.

She frequently asked herself, "How could a young kid outwit me, a seasoned criminal and trained detective? It just didn't make sense!"

She surmised he'd gone underground or taken on a new identity like herself. Maybe he'd even skipped town by now, she considered. None of these thoughts gave her any pleasure. She wanted to see him behind bars – her bars!

Just as she was running out of possible

ideas on where to flush out Finn, her assistant knocked on her office door.

"I think you might want to take this call from a Kiwi Taxi Company driver."

Strong picked up the phone, and after a short conversation with the caller, she jumped out of her chair, grabbed her white police hat, jammed it on her head, and barked orders to her assistant.

"The taxi driver just took Finn to the Suez Yacht Club with some old guy. He recognized his face from the Fugitive Alert. Get the police helicopter ready for an emergency flight to the Suez Yacht Club! And contact the Deputy Director at Interpol Cairo. Tell him to alert their border patrol staff in Suez to prepare their police boat for a possible chase."

She rubbed her hands together. "I'm coming for you, Finn. This time you can't slip away from my grip!"

A few minutes later, the border patrol office

in Suez got the emergency message. The office clerk made a rush trip to the local office supply store for a new printer cartridge, so they could print out the Fugitive Alert information about Finn. They quickly distributed copies to the members of their local police force. Their police boat had a full tank of gas. They were ready for a pursuit on the water.

Sarge and Finn didn't notice of the docked Interpol police boat as they entered the office of the Suez Yacht Club.

Sarge thought, "I know I'm not going to get the keys to the *Quest* without a hefty baksheesh to the port captain."

Luckily the port captain was happy to take the wad of money and look the other way. Sarge and Finn hastened to board the *Quest,* so they could leave the port as fast as possible.

"Finn, store our bags below deck, and get ready to help me gas up this beauty."

"Got it!"

Finn was below deck a long time. Sarge steered the boat to the gas pump to fill up the tank, all the while hoping Finn wasn't getting cold feet.

Suddenly Sarge noticed a police helicopter landing on the Yacht Club roof -- not a good sign.

"Finn, what are you doing down there? We're about to take off."

Just then, Finn came above deck holding a strange looking device.

"Sarge, do you have any idea what this is?"

Sarge grabbed the device to be sure he saw clearly.

"It's an electromagnetic device jammer! This device is the insurance we need to fend off any other boats pursuing us. A jammer like this can shut down the electrical system of another boat up to 600 feet away!"

Sarge wasn't surprised that Strong would have something this devious to protect herself at sea. Lucky for them!

"Finn, you just struck gold! Store that device below deck where you can grab it quickly. It will help keep us safe."

Just then Sarge caught sight of the Interpol police boat coming towards them with Detective Strong at the helm. His face froze.

"Hang on, Finn. Our takeoff is going to be exciting!"

Sarge gunned the *Quest*'s engines and sped away from the dock.

From what Sarge could see, the Interpol Police boat was about 28-feet long, and it had only one outboard engine. He guessed it could reach about 50 mph, so he accelerated the *Quest* to 60 mph for about 15 minutes, and then cut her engines back to 40 mph to conserve gas.

Thanks to Sarge, the Interpol Police boat

was soon a speck in the *Quest's* wake.

Finn hollered to Sarge over the din of the engines, "We've outrun them! We didn't even have to use the electromagnetic device jammer. Saved from Strong's clutches once again!"

Sarge nodded to Finn, "We'll have to watch our backs for the entire voyage. Stay sharp!"

Strong blamed herself for not being able to catch the *Quest*. She slunk back to Cairo where she kept in daily contact with the Interpol Police and the Eastern Africa Police Chiefs Cooperation Organization (EAPCCO).

The sea chase had just begun!

Finn took to the sea in a way that surprised him. He basked in feeling the warm sun, breathing in the salt air, and feeling the water spray on his face and over his shoes. The best part of all was when Sarge wasn't watching him, which was most of the time. No one could see him. Finn loved the boating life compared to his former life of sneaking and thieving through crowded alleyways.

Sarge lived up to his word. So far, he safely navigated the *Quest* over 3,000 miles with 13 uneventful stops along the coasts of Egypt, Sudan, Eritrea, Djibouti, Somalia, and Kenya to refuel and replenish their supplies.

Finn started to drop his guard. By their second week at sea, he felt safe for the first time in a long time. That is until the day they left the port of Tanga, Tanzania.

As he scanned the horizon that overcast morning, Finn realized that someone was watching him!

Three sleek, black speedboats zipped toward the *QUEST* at full speed.

"Sarge!?!" Finn hollered.

"Shut up already! I'm standing right behind you."

Finn whirled around to see Sarge standing behind him, with his slicker billowing in the west wind.

"Interpol is coming for us!" shrieked Finn.

Sarge grabbed Finn by the shoulders.

"That's not Interpol or Strong. They wouldn't use boats such as those for the green notice they sent out on us."

"Green notice?" asked Finn.

"An Interpol notice level. It provides warnings about persons who have committed criminal offenses and are likely to repeat these crimes in other countries," explained Sarge.

"Oh, crap," muttered Finn.

Sarge looked closer at the oncoming vessels.

"Those are pirates! Get the jammer!"

Finn headed quickly below deck, tripping down the slippery stairs. He soon reappeared, lugging the electromagnetic device jammer.

About three minutes later a blue pulse slammed out from the *Quest's* hull and rippled into the ships that were now about 30 yards away. The vessels stopped in their wakes.

For his signature move, Finn stood motionless at the *Quest's* stern. Three playing cards whisked out Finn's sleeve, and in a fluid motion, they flew into the air whirling in distinct arcs into the three pirate captains' hands.

Sarge gaped at Finn.

"Kid, your card trick was impressive. You've used your downtime on the *Quest* to your advantage!"

The unlikely pair of fugitives laughed at the pirates' shouts of frustration and annoyance as the *Quest* sped away.

A few hours later, there was a bellow from the bow.

"Finn!" called Sarge. "We're coming up on Dar es Salaam in a few hours! Go get some sleep!"

Finn obliged. As he was going below deck, he saw a mark on the horizon, like a leak in a ball point pen, but more prominent! A storm!

"Sarge!" he called out. "Look!"

"Crap! We'll need to head toward Zanzibar City, fast!" commanded Sarge.

The storm hit them about fifteen minutes later when they were still approximately 10 miles from Zanzibar City. The rain flooded below deck and weighed them down. Waves upon waves of water and fish splashed overboard, creating slippery and dangerous conditions on deck. The two sailors were in serious trouble.

Sarge used a hose to bail out the water. He

hooked it up to a contraption that collected water from below deck.

"I now hate the sea!" Finn yelled over the pounding waves against the *Quest's* hull.

To himself, he cried, "I could have stayed behind in Cairo and survived incognito in an alleyway for crying out loud! Why did I agree to this never-ending voyage?"

Above the din of the storm, Finn hollered to Sarge, "Why can't we get a minute of dryness here?!?"

"I think you have the answer to your prayers, Finn. We're about to enter the eye of the storm, snapped Sarge.

"If you shut up and pay attention for a second you'll see what I mean. Zanzibar is in our sights. We can dock there and get some fresh supplies and clean clothes."

"Well come on then! Let's get to port!" Finn shrieked.

9

A CLOSE CALL

After a short respite when the *Quest* sat in the eye of the storm, soon she was again at the mercy of the strong wind and blinding rain. From what Sarge could see through the relentless downpour, the actual port of Zanzibar City had changed little since he docked there with the British Navy several decades ago.

About 3:00 a.m., Sarge cautiously approached the dock and pulled the *Quest* in next to a tender from the imposing Greek Navy ship they passed in the outer harbor. He recalled seeing such a Greek frigate in the Red Sea during Operation Desert Storm.

Those were flashbacks for another day.

Sarge didn't want Finn to know of his concern that the storm was a bad omen for them. The *Quest* was intact but battered from the ordeal, and they had hundreds of miles to go before reaching Madagascar. He knew that neither of them would be deterred — himself because he loved a sea adventure and Finn because he needed closure on what had happened to his parents.

With a joint effort, they tied the *Quest* to a mooring. The rain and wind started to abate, and they took refuge below deck to wait until morning when they could take stock of their worrisome situation.

The next morning Sarge was up early — the skies had nearly cleared. He checked out the *Quest*. It seemed seaworthy, but their clothes were soaked, and their food was inedible. Time to wake the kid.

"Finn, haul your butt on deck!"

Finn woke with a start. The night before was a nightmare. He didn't know anything about where they had landed. He was just glad to be relatively dry and in port – any port!

"Kid, we need to take stock, gas up, get new supplies, and move on as fast as possible."

Sarge recalculated their route.

Zanzibar City, Tanzania > Mtwara,
Tanzania ....**294 miles**

Mtwara, Tanzania > Bouenindi,
Comoros ....**228 miles**

Bouendini, Comoros > Mtsamboro,
Mayotte ....**144 miles**

Mtsamboro, Mayott > Anorotsangana, Madagascar
....**209 miles**

He was relieved they only had 875 miles to go --small change compared to the distance they already navigated through the Red Sea and the Gulf of Aden.

They hadn't lost much in mileage with this unexpected detour into Zanzibar City. He would have been happy to spare them the terror of navigating through the horrendous storm. But now he knew the kid was seaworthy.

The two sailors got busy making a list of what they needed to get them to Madagascar. Thankfully, the cash in their metal box stayed dry.

Neither of them wanted to think about what lay ahead once they reached that mysterious island. Their fear of the unknown might overtake their determination to proceed.

"We're going to town together. It's not safe for us to separate. We're going to wait until dark to reduce our chances of being spotted," cautioned Sarge.

Finn was feeling hungry and queasy simultaneously. He was so disoriented after their harrowing night that he meekly complied with Sarge's order. The only thing to do was to go back below deck and get some more rest. Finn passed out. Sarge nodded off with one eye open.

Sarge awoke at dusk. To be prepared for a quick getaway, he quietly gassed up the *Quest* for the next leg of their trip.

He shook Finn. "Time to go, kid."

Together, they stealthily moved from the dock to land and then onto the nearby dusty road.

Sarge remembered from his experience in Zanzibar City that the dala dala taxi was the only public transportation in the city. If they waited beside the road, it would eventually pick them up and take them to the shopping area. After about a 30-minute wait, a rickety and crowded converted lorry stopped to give them a lift. They were thankful to travel under a black starless sky.

Sarge took advantage of their slow and bumpy ride into town to school Finn about Zanzibar City.

"We're actually on the western side of an island called Unguja," remarked Sarge.

"You'll be surprised when you see the city," continued Sarge. "It smells of spices, fish, and seaweed. Most of the population is Muslim, so you'll feel right at home with the sound of the minarets. The mosques aren't nearly as ornate as the ones you've seen in Cairo. Like any city, there's a large disparity between the wealthy and the poor."

"The first thing I want to do is get something to eat," exclaimed Finn. "My stomach is too empty to growl!"

"Ok, but let me do all the talking," instructed Sarge, who wondered if Finn grasped anything he just told him about Zanzibar City.

Together they walked through the shopping

district, which was still alive at night. By 9:00 p.m., they had purchased new seaworthy wardrobes and much-needed food. Thankfully, the *Quest* had a watermaker for converting sea water to potable water. They stopped at an outside stall to fill their stomachs with BBQ chicken and roasted sweet potatoes. Finally, the wary duo caught the next dala dala back to port.

As they approached their dock, Sarge grabbed Finn by the shoulder and spun him around.

"What are you doing?" screamed Finn.

Sarge put his hand over Finn's mouth, which only fueled the boy's fears. He pulled Finn behind the port administration building. Only then did Sarge take his rough hand off the boy's face.

"Listen, kid. There's an Interpol guard by the *Quest*. They've spotted us!"

Finn froze, with his thoughts racing.

"There has to be a way out! We've come this far – there's no turning back!"

Within seconds, Finn had a plan.

"Sarge, I spotted a laundry bag with clean Greek Navy uniforms near the tender tied up next to the *Quest*. I'll swim under the dock, pull up for a minute, grab the bag, and then swim back, holding it over my head to keep it dry."

"Can you do it without making a ripple or a sound to alert the guard?"

"You know me. I'm a pro at thievery!"

"Ok, go for it, but be quick."

Sarge waited nervously behind the building while Finn went on his mission. If he succeeded, they might just escape Zanzibar City. If he failed, they quickly needed to create Plan B. He held his breath.

Suddenly there was a thud – a laundry bag flew and hit Sarge on the head. He didn't duck fast enough, but he recovered in a flash.

Luckily there were enough uniform pieces of the right size in the bag to outfit both Finn and Sarge. Never were there two more mismatched members of the Greek Navy! They donned white blouses and trousers. After Sarge gave Finn a helping hand knotting and straightening his long navy uniform tie, they both pulled the soft white caps over their eyes.

They knew they couldn't linger on the dock in case Interpol decided to supplement the guard near the *Quest.* They decided to stash their bags of food and clothing behind the administration building, hoping their supplies would be safe until their return.

Sarge and Finn hopped on the next dala dala that appeared. During the ride to town, they quietly discussed their plan.

By the time the sailors reached Zanzibar City for the second time that night, it was about 11:00 p.m. Sarge and Finn found an all-night coffee shop. They tried to be nonobtrusive by keeping their heads down reading local magazines and newspapers. There weren't many coffee drinkers at that hour. Hopefully, it wasn't a favorite spot of the local Interpol police!

Finn couldn't stifle his yawns. It had been an exciting and an exhausting 24 hours.

"Keep your mind on why you hired Sarge to take you to Madagascar," he thought to himself.

Sarge focused on his reading material, or maybe he slept. Finn couldn't be sure.

Suddenly, there was a loud crackle, and the lights went out! The two imposters quickly ran outside with the few other people from the coffee shop and saw that the whole city was blacked out!

"Kid, the gods are with us! Let's go!"

The sleepy dala dala driver didn't expect to have many fares late at night, but she was happy to have the company of two rumpled looking Greek sailors.

"I guess they had quite a night on the town," she chuckled to herself.

When they reached the dock, Sarge pulled Finn behind the pitch-dark administration building.

Sarge whispered to Finn, "I'm going to throw the guard off the dock. When I give you the signal, come running to the *Quest* with our supplies. Be quick. We have a full tank of gas, and we can leave port before he can pull himself out of the water and blow the whistle on us. Got it?"

Finn nodded with enthusiasm. He loved a caper of any size. This one was getting more exciting by the minute.

He crouched down and kept quiet behind the administration building, as Sarge had instructed. Finn's ears perked in anticipation of the signal. Did he just hear a loud cry and a big splash?

"Finn, move it!" hollered Sarge.

Finn grabbed the bags and ran down the dock. He heaved the bags to Sarge, jumped on board the *Quest*, and untied the ropes from their mooring. Sarge revved the engines. With mutual relief, they hunkered down in the boat and headed to their next gas stop, Mtwara, Tanzania, about 300 miles from Zanzibar City.

Finn would never forget their exciting adventure in Zanzibar City.

Strong received two calls from Interpol in Zanzibar City. The first message was the one she'd been waiting to receive. Sarge and Finn were in the port of Zanzibar City, and Interpol would pick them up as soon as they returned to the *Quest*. They posted their most experienced guard on the dock.

The second call was the one she'd been dreading. Once again, Sarge and Finn escaped. She had a very uneasy feeling that Madagascar was their destination. They could discover her dark secret about her criminal background if they're as smart as Strong thinks they are. She had no choice but to act fast.

Strong flew to Zanzibar. She hired a large chase boat with a crew of 10 and charted their course to Madagascar. With every hour that elapsed, Strong's worry mounted. She believed Sarge and Finn might head close to the scene of her past crime.

Sarge and Finn were oblivious to being pursued by Strong and her crew on their 110-foot boat with a top speed of 29 mph and a range of 3300 miles.

The fugitives knew Strong was a formidable

adversary. But this time they didn't foresee that she had a reliable boat to match her equally firm intention of capturing them.

A coast guard trawler spotted the *Quest* en route to Madagascar and radioed their coordinates to Strong. The coast guard vessel couldn't chase the *Quest* because they had a severely injured sailor on board. The ship needed to go in the opposite direction for medical aid. It was now up to Strong and her crew to capture the *Quest* and the two elusive thieves.

After several more days navigating the Indian Ocean and stopping for gas in Tanzania and on the islands of Comoros and Mayotte, Sarge and Finn were nearing their destination, the northeast coast of Madagascar. Unbeknownst to them, Strong and her crew were right behind them, quickly closing the nautical gap.

10

THE DEADLY STING

Finn awoke from a deep sleep. He lay still in that space between sleep and wakefulness. He could sense questions not yet asked. Gradually they began to surface in his consciousness. The answers didn't appear. Ambiguity was frustrating at times.

"What's happening?" he mused.

As he lay on his bunk, Finn realized that the *Quest* was not slicing through the water. The engines were no longer running at 80 mph. He didn't know how long he slept.

Abruptly, a call from above deck subdued one of his emerging questions.

"Finn! You've slept for three and a half hours! Know what that means?" hollered Sarge.

"No idea!" he answered.

"Then haul your ass up here and see for yourself!"

Finn scrambled up on deck and held his breath as he absorbed the visual panorama. They had arrived! The multi-shades of the green jungle of Madagascar spread out behind a rocky cliff outlining the pristine white beach.

"I wonder what the water's like," Finn mused.

Sarge knew Finn was just trying to get acclimated.

"Why don't we find out?" Sarge answered.

"Huh?"

Then Sarge pushed Finn overboard.

"AHHHHHHH" Finn screamed.

He belly-flopped into the water, making a dramatic splash.

"I thought you said **we** would find out!" Finn spluttered.

"I did, you test it and tell me, and we'll both know," Sarge wisecracked.

"Swim to shore, and I'll get this baby closer to the beach as well."

Ten minutes later Sarge and Finn were standing on the beach with their bare feet dug into the sand. The sun was ablaze in its high noon position.

"So, Finn, what's your plan?" Sarge questioned.

"Tomorrow morning we'll go into town and gather any info we can."

Sarge smirked. "You know the town's an hour or two away on foot, right? We can stay out of sight on this concealed beach."

"Why did we land so far away from the nearest town?" Finn asked his partner.

"Do I need to remind you we're wanted criminals on the run? Do you expect me to dock at a swanky beach close to a resort hotel? Strong can't find us as easily here," Sarge countered.

Finn knew he couldn't win that argument.

"Then we can start our research in the local newspaper office, using assumed names."

"How do you know they'd have any info about your parents or that they even have a local town newspaper?" responded Sarge.

"I don't!" Finn cheerfully responded.

"Whatever, go get some firewood," Sarge ordered.

"Hookeley-Dokeley!" Finn responded.

"Did you seriously just say that?"

"I was imitating Ned Flanders from *The Simpsons*!"

As Finn was returning with an armful of kindling, he heard a shout and then a loud thump. He slammed through the thick foliage and catapulted from the tree line to find Sarge laying on the sand with an angry red puncture wound on his right calf.

Out of the corner of his eye, Finn caught sight of a sizable crimson-black scorpion crawling away from his wounded partner.

11

THE TRUTH OF THE JUNGLE

Finn ran to Sarge's convulsing body.

"Sarge! Don't pass out!" screamed Finn.

Finn gently lifted Sarge's sagging head and poured a trickle of water down his throat. Sarge involuntarily spat it out into Finn's face. With a guttural moan, Sarge passed out in Finn's arms.

Finn could see the site of the bite was already red and swelling. As Finn held Sarge, he felt him twitch and could sense he was having difficulty breathing.

The enormity of his situation hit Finn like a typhoon. His navigator was spiraling towards death, Finn was unable to operate the *Quest* solo to go for help, and Detective Strong and Interpol were possibly still on their trail.

Shaking with sheer terror, Finn started talking to himself, so he could get a grip on the situation.

"Ok, what are my options? There's no way I'm going to let Sarge die on this God-forsaken beach. I have to get help, and I have to move fast!"

Finn looked around, taking in the beach, the *Quest,* and the jungle.

"Our only hope is for me to hike into the dense vegetation and get medical help from the locals."

Feeling more frightened than he had ever felt in his life, Finn grabbed his backpack and began filling it with food, water, Sarge's military knife, and the flashlight from the *Quest*. He saw that Sarge was breathing with a lot of effort. He hadn't moved from the spot where the scorpion bit him.

"Sarge, you can't hear me, but if you regain consciousness while I'm gone, drink this water and eat this food I'm leaving for you. Hopefully, you'll know that I'm bringing help and you'll hang on until I return."

With tearful eyes and shaking knees, Finn strapped on his backpack and picked a spot to start his trek into the unknown jungle. He had to trust that his ingenuity had gotten him this far, and it would guide him to find the right people to help Sarge in time.

"Oh, God, please let me get back to Sarge in time," prayed Finn, as he ventured into the ominous-looking jungle.

"When did I start to believe in prayer?" he questioned.

By now it was early afternoon. Finn recalled Sarge's words that the nearest town was an hour or two away. But in which direction? There was no way to know for sure.

"Even if I must hike clear across Madagascar, I'm going to get help for Sarge!"

His street smarts kicked in, and Finn realized he needed to mark his trail, so he could find his way back to the beach. He started to notch the trees with Sarge's knife as he took his first steps into the dark terrain.

With tentative steps, Finn put some distance between himself and his injured partner, who remained unconscious and oblivious to his peril. Finn found it challenging and scary to hike through the jungle alone. Whenever he felt thirsty or tired he stopped to drink or eat, but not for long. Sarge's life depended on him!

As the sun started to set, the noises in the jungle became deafening. Finn hoped he would find help before dark, but it was not to be the case. The underbrush tore his pants. The humidity drenched his shirt in sweat. He continued to mark the trees and was relieved to observe he wasn't hiking in circles.

By dusk, Finn's state of mind was beyond fear for himself and concern for Sarge. His prime focus was on his survival of the nighttime jungle terrors.

"What are those shadows?" Finn whispered.

His knees knocked, but he continued to press forward. Just as the relentless sun met the horizon, he spotted the outline of a single structure in the shape of a yurt covered with a dark felt-like material.

Although there was no sign of life around the dwelling, Finn approached it carefully and quietly. He didn't want any surprises. By the time the boy found the entrance on the far side of the shelter, he was sure no one was living there. With a massive sigh of relief, he dropped onto the floor of the yurt and fell asleep on his backpack.

"Where am I?" Finn wondered when he opened his eyes the next morning.

He was unaware of the bats watching him from the roofline of the yurt.

There was no time to speculate. Finn checked his body for scratches and found he had only minor injuries from his first solo day in the jungle. He couldn't ignore his grumbling stomach and dry mouth. The terrifying image of Sarge passed out on the beach prompted him to jump up, grab his water bottle and a bit of food, and pick a new direction for day two.

"Hopefully I'll find a sign of life today, and I can get medical help for Sarge!"

With those words of self-encouragement, Finn hastily set out and ventured even further into the jungle, notching the trees along the way.

Sometimes the jungle was quiet, and Finn could see a sliver of gray sky overhead. More often, though, he heard a cacophony of sounds from birds, insects, and monkeys and unidentified jungle inhabitants – some close and others calling from a distance.

He passed two small graves and couldn't help but wonder about their story. The two mounds were not the sign of life he was hoping to find.

He couldn't lose his nerve. Sarge's life was at stake. He never expected to be such a world away from the busy Cairo bazaar, where he thrived as a petty thief. This solo journey was testing his old survival skills and forcing him to develop new ones along the way.

Finn fell into a hypnotic state as he trudged through the damp and unforgiving jungle. On the second day of his mission, he sensed he was no closer to the nearest village or town than he was on the previous day. No matter – he would just keep putting one foot in front of the other.

"Oh, crap here comes the rain!" complained Finn, as he held his face upward to catch some of the cooling drops.

How quickly the jungle turned from daylight to darkness with pelting sheets of rain falling in every direction.

As if the sudden turn in the weather wasn't enough of a cause for alarm, Finn heard a high-pitched screeching noise. He scanned the treetops and saw a family of monkeys following his every move. He swung around to holler at them and without warning lost his footing.

The sensation of falling 20 feet down into a dark jungle cave is one that never left Finn for the rest of his life. He thought he knew what fear felt like, but when his mouth opened to let out a scream, he was unable to make a sound.

Thud! Finn landed on the hard surface of the jungle cave floor. He tentatively felt his arms and legs and found everything intact.

"Backpack?" Finn uttered.

He reached around his body until he found the familiar lump of his backpack and slowly pulled it towards him.

"Oh, God, please let my flashlight work!"

There's that unfamiliar feeling again of praying!

Holding the flashlight beam steady, Finn examined his new surroundings. The cave was dark and damp, but luckily there was no sign of bats or other jungle creatures.

As he panned the light around the cave walls, Finn spotted a small pile of papers and a few small boxes. He tiptoed closer to the area and scrutinized the debris with his flashlight before moving any closer.

"Somebody else has been in this cave...that's a relief, in a way," Finn supposed.

At the bottom of one of the boxes, Finn uncovered an ancient jungle map. Sarge told him that Madagascar was a primary trade route in the late 18th and early 19th centuries. Is it possible that this delicate document leads to buried treasure?

Finn stuffed the map in his backpack with the hope that Sarge could shed some light on it.

Next, he uncovered some old newspaper clippings about an archeological theft. A sophisticated thieving ring stole valuable artifacts from a highly regarded academic married couple called Campbell -- Finn's parents!

"What! The lead suspect in the theft is Simone Spivey!! That's Amanda Strong in that photo!! What!!!"

"She's an imposter and a thief!! Wait until Sarge sees this!!"

Then it hit Finn. This stuff belonged to his parents. Those two graves were theirs. He hung his head.

The truth was -- his parents were looking

for gold treasure in this Madagascar jungle and met untimely deaths.

Finn didn't want to think about how they died. He was only relieved to know their fate and to be able to retrieve what he could from their belongings.

There wasn't much left to sort through, only one other small box. Feeling dejected, Finn kicked it open. Inside the box was a medicine vial. He read the statement on the box flap:

The Food and Drug Administration approves this medication, Anascorp, specifically for scorpion stings. Scorpion stings can be life-threatening and can cause loss of muscle control and difficulty breathing, requiring heavy sedation and intensive care in a hospital. Administer without delay after a scorpion sting.

"Holy cow! I've got to get this to Sarge today!"

Finn's spirits lifted as he realized he now

knew the fate of his parents. He uncovered a preserved antidote to counteract Sarge's sting. He might have a treasure map stuffed in his backpack. He carried evidence that Strong was an imposter. His prayers were answered and then some!

All he needed now was to find a way out of the cave, so he could retrace his jungle path back to Sarge to save his life!

"There has to be a way out of here!" Finn's shouts echoed off the walls of the cave

12

THE RETREAT

Strong provided seven of her hired crew members with weapons before they left the cruiser. After anchoring the rented boat about a mile offshore, they landed its dinghy on the secluded beach. The energized group secured the dinghy with a pile of rocks and prepared to continue their pursuit of Finn and Sarge.

"Let's move it!" Strong ordered as she and her posse jogged down the beach.

"Wait. What's that?" one of the crew members shouted.

There was a dark speck on the beach ahead near the rocks at the base of the cliff. They all ran toward it.

"Sarge!" exclaimed Strong.

He looked ill though. No matter, they'd treat him back in the cruiser. Strong was determined to take him back alive.

"Throw him in the dinghy. I'll take Graham with me to track down Finn. You six -- Matt, Pete, Rich, Conor, Jimmy, and Gus -- stay here in case he comes back from another direction," commanded Strong.

The crew members obeyed Strong's commands without questions.

Strong and Graham hadn't traveled very far into the jungle when they came across a moldy dwelling. There was an old man calmly rocking on a chair on the hut's slanted porch.

"Sir, can you tell me if you've seen a kid with a backpack run by here recently?"

"Can't say I have, can't say I haven't. I see

many things around this vanilla bean farm. Might need something to jog my memory if you know what I mean," the rocking man answered.

She did know what he meant. She slipped him a 10,000Ar note.

"I know that he has a backpack."

"I already knew that!"

"Then I forgot again. Need another memory jogger."

By now Strong was frustrated.

"Here!"

She thrust another 10,000Ar note at him.

"Now, have you seen him or not?"

"Nope, no idea who you're talking about."

"Oh, for crying out loud!!!"

She and Graham stormed off.

Five minutes later they came to another farm.

"No, wait. What? We're back at the same hut," Storm seethed.

"You just traveled in a circle!" the man hollered.

They set off again but arrived at the same farm for the third time!

Finally, the rocking man took pity on them.

"I'll tell you how to get out of that crazy jungle loop! Well, I would, but I seem to have forgotten how. Cough. *20,000Ar*. Cough. Cough."

After paying the old farmer for the third time, Strong and Graham reluctantly retreated to the beach to set a trap for Finn.

13

THE BIG TRADE

Finn's flashlight began to flicker. He didn't dare replace the batteries if he could still see even the slightest bit of light in the dark and damp cave. He had to conserve everything – his energy, food, water, battery power, and most important, the salvaged documents stuffed in his backpack.

Not only would he expose Amanda Strong as the fraudster she is, but his days of street thievery would be over if he and Sarge discovered the gold treasure.

"I have to get out of this cave and fast!" he declared aloud.

Nighttime fell in the silent and shadowy cave. Finn hadn't seen Sarge for two days, and there was no telling about the tough vet's condition since he got that nasty scorpion sting.

"Sarge, stay conscious. You can't leave me now!" implored Finn from his subterranean dungeon.

There were corners in the cave where Finn couldn't stand, but he continued to explore every angle for a possible exit. What he thought was another flicker from his fading flashlight caused him to take a double-take. That flickering light was coming from a different source. He looked up and spotted a faint beam of light through the crevice in the roof of the cave.

Finn hunched over and followed the crack of light into the next section of the cave. His feet started to feel warm, and he realized he was standing in a flood zone!

"Maybe this is a good sign," Finn conjectured.

"If there is light above and water below, then the crevice might get bigger ahead, and I can find my way out of this God-forsaken place."

Squish, squish. Finn kept trudging forward while shining his dim flashlight on the roof of the cave. After a few minutes, he spotted a larger opening above – one he thought he could reach and squeak through. The light of the full moon was in his favor.

First, he boosted himself up on a slippery ledge and heaved his backpack over his head and out through the narrow opening in the rocks.

Success!

Now, to get himself free. Everything Finn needed to keep himself and Sarge alive was in that backpack. Once again, there was no Plan B.

Finn had flashbacks to all those days of perfecting his agility in the crowded Cairo bazaar. He imagined himself applying his skill to perform what looked like an impossible feat.

Being careful to find the least soaked portion of the narrow ledge, Finn pulled himself up. He searched with his hands until he found another small shelf above his head where he could boost himself through the escape route.

"It's now or never. One, two, three!" yelled Finn.

He pulled himself up on the shelf and threw himself through the crack. It was a narrow escape. Finn's skinny body just fit through the opening. On the outside, he fell into a patch of jungle undergrowth. Thankfully it was a soft landing.

He found his backpack and fished out the extra batteries to repower the flashlight. He figured if he moved fast, it would take him about one and a half days to work his way back to Sarge.

"Thank goodness I notched the trees!"

exclaimed Finn with great relief.

The two graves held a whole new meaning for Finn when he retraced his steps through the jungle. He stopped and spoke with his parents.

"I don't know what happened to you two, but I want you to know you have a son that will see your mission through. The thieves who stole your hard-won artifacts will get their punishment. Sarge and I will complete your goal to unearth the gold treasure in this jungle. You don't know Sarge, my partner in adventure, but I promise you'll be proud of us. I don't know what else to say except that I'll be back with Sarge and I'll let you know how it's going with our search for the gold."

Feeling recharged for the first time in a long time, Finn set out again through the humid jungle. Soon the now familiar yurt came into view. This time, he could only stop for a brief rest. Sarge's life was in his hands, literally and figuratively, with the precious antidote for the scorpion sting in his rank backpack.

As dusk approached, Finn felt spent from hours of pushing himself forward in the steamy and unforgiving jungle. He sensed a change in the terrain.

"I must be getting close to the beach!" breathed Finn.

He picked up his pace, as he continuously flashed his light off and on to alert Sarge of his approach. Finn pushed from his mind any possibility that Sarge was dead. He would only entertain the image of his being unconscious or delirious. At the same time, he knew he had to get to him pronto.

Finn's arch enemy, Amanda Strong, along with Graham, were on surveillance for any sign of him in the jungle perimeter around Sarge's lifeless body lying in the dinghy. Finn's flashing light was the sign they needed to jump into action to catch their prey.

"It's over, Finn!" Strong screamed as she

threw herself into his path, pistol drawn.

Graham stood by her with his hand on his holster.

Finn's heart stopped, and he fell to his knees.

"Maybe Strong has finally beaten us," he thought glumly.

Suddenly an eerie, wailing call sounded through the jungle undergrowth. It was a cross between a police siren and a humpback whale. Finn looked around. Strong didn't move; she kept her weapon pointed at Finn.

In a matter of a few seconds after their hearing the wailing call, dozens of small, brown lemurs surrounded Strong and Graham and threw them off balance. Before she had time even to take in what was happening, Strong fell on her butt, with her feet flailing in the air like an overturned turtle. Graham suffered a similar fate.

Detective Strong's police-issue Beretta M9 flew high above her head and then landed about five yards away in the dense jungle foliage. Finn saw his chance and took off like a shot through the nearest clearing. He didn't stop to retrieve the weapon. He had a single purpose -- to get to Sarge with the antidote as fast as possible.

Strong didn't flail on her back for long. She quickly regained her balance, found her gun, and fired a few shots in the air to scare away the lemurs. They ran in terror. Graham was slow to get up, feeling dazed by the quick turn of events.

Soon Finn, Strong, and Graham were in a foot race to the beach. The pursuers chased Finn through an area where he had not notched the trees. He was quickly losing his bearings.

There was a ravine ahead. Finn counted on his young legs giving him the advantage over Strong and Graham. He was right. He jumped the ditch with no problem, while Strong and Graham had to find a narrower crossing.

"Crap! That looks like another cave pit ahead." Finn breathed in alarm.

"I won't fall into a trap this time."

Finn quickly darted to the right to avoid the cave pit. He sensed that he had left Strong and Graham behind on the other side of the ravine. Now, to circle back around and get to the beach.

Finn flickered his flashlight again. He was very quiet – hoping to hear or smell the salt water.

"I'm getting close," he exclaimed, quickening his pace.

Soon Finn saw some familiar notched trees and quickly rerouted himself to the beach. He'll never forget what he saw when he emerged from the jungle and reached the beach.

"I'm coming, Sarge," yelled Finn, as he

leaped onto the sand.

There was Sarge, prone in the dinghy on the rocky beach, alive and semi-conscious and looking very weak. Strong and her armed crew members surrounded him.

"How did she beat me back here?"

Finn would never stop asking himself this question. No answer made sense.

As Finn scanned the scene, he knew he had to think fast to disarm Strong.

"Detective Strong, before I surrender, I would like to speak with you privately," requested Finn.

Amanda was quite surprised at Finn's request, but the word, 'surrender,' brought a smile to her face.

"Sure, kid. My crew will train their weapons on us while we talk."

Strong and Finn stepped away from the

group.

Finn spoke softly. "Detective, I'm sure you don't want anyone in your party to hear this, so I'll whisper. Listen carefully. In my backpack, I have proof of your role in the unsolved art and artifact theft from my parents, the Campbells.

"In the cave near my parents' graves, I found the documents proving your shady past. I'll expose you as the despicable imposter you are to the authorities at Interpol and the Cairo Police Department unless you agree to make this deal.

"You give me Sarge, and I'll give you the cash box and the *Quest*. You must return to Cairo and call off your obsession to chase us for all time. We plan to remain on the island indefinitely. Those are my terms. Do you have any questions?"

Strong's face dripped in disbelief. She gasped for air. The tables had turned without warning, and now her life was on the block.

Detective Strong immediately knew her only choice was to concede. She nodded affirmatively to Finn and walked over to the crew members, who guarded Finn and Sarge.

"Weapons down. We're pulling out. Madagascar has an immunity law that protects these criminals. Just my bad luck."

After handing her the cash box, Finn turned his back on Strong and her crew as they dumped Sarge's body on the beach, hitched the dinghy to the *Quest*, and headed out to the anchored cruiser.

"Good riddance," spewed Finn.

Sarge started to moan, "What's happening?

"You've been stung by a scorpion."

With that understatement, Finn administered the antidote and waited for Sarge to regain consciousness.

"Do you want the good news or the good

news first?" Finn asked Sarge coyly.

After Finn updated Sarge on the events of the last 36 hours, Sarge was in awe of Finn.

"Well, partner," started Sarge. "At least you found your parents' graves. I'm sorry you had to discover them by yourself."

"I'm going to finish their work, with your help. All we have to do now is find the gold treasure. I have what looks like a treasure map in my backpack. We can study it together when you're feeling stronger."

"All we have are the shirts on our backs, but we're plenty resourceful," countered Sarge.

Finn grabbed his backpack and pulled out wads and wads of cash.

"It's a shame Strong didn't look under the top layer of bills in the cash box before she left. We'll probably hear her scream from here when she discovers she fell for my amateur trick."

14

A FORTUNE IN GOLD

While Sarge slowly recovered from the scorpion sting, he had time to consider the state of his partnership with Finn.

"I can't call him Kid anymore. Finn proved he's a man in a boy's body. He skipped the whole teenage thing. He's a hero. I owe him my life. We'll be mates forever," thought Sarge.

Finn convinced Sarge that they should set up base camp in the abandoned yurt. Sarge got on board with the idea when Finn pointed out that no scorpions were crawling out from under beach rocks there. They took their cash and bought new supplies and local maps. Then they set up their base camp in the musty yurt.

For several weeks, the fortune-hunters studied the local maps along with the treasure map. Each day they set out in a new direction and trudged through the jungle, getting the lay of the land.

"I'm not a big fan of bugs and rain and relentless humidity, and I must be crazy, but this search sure beats marking time on my airless roof in Cairo," commented Sarge on one of their sweltering reconnaissance hikes.

Sarge, wiping his dripping brow, took a respite on a big rock, while Finn hiked ahead with the maps in hand.

"Sarge!" hollered Finn.

Sarge grabbed his pack and ran to meet up with Finn. Even though it was high noon, the jungle floor was dark and slippery. Sarge heard his partner shout again.

"Over here! Hurry!"

As the big, wet leaves parted in front of his

face, Sarge was stunned. Finn was encircled by about a hundred natives, who didn't look all that friendly. They were mostly adults, with a few teenagers and kids peering from the tree branches.

Sarge eased his way closer to the circle and kept a big, foolish smile on his face, hoping to signal their friendly intentions. The natives weren't buying it.

The leader stepped closer to Finn. Sarge held back outside the circle.

The leader spoke. "We've been watching you two with your maps and notes, searching for something on our land. Who are you and what are you doing here?"

"We're archaeologists from Cairo University," Finn said with assurance.

"Two of our colleagues started an expedition here and didn't return. We're here to finish their mission. I'm Finn Campbell, and this is Sarge, pointing to his accomplice," explained Finn.

"I remember your colleagues. They brought some much-needed medical help to our village. Their deaths brought great sadness to my people," commented the leader.

"What's your name?" asked Finn

"I'm Tanjona."

"Do you have any objection to our finishing their archaeology dig? We're just trying to find the right spot before we break ground. And we're going to need some help, so there's work in it for your tribesmen."

Sarge restrained himself. Finn was a master at slithering out of tight spots. It was best to let him take the lead.

"I'll give you fourteen sunsets to finish your search for the right spot. If you don't find it by then, you must leave. If you do find it, then we'll meet again and listen to your plan."

"Agreed," said Finn, with relief.

The natives barely acknowledged Sarge as they withdrew into the jungle. They accepted Finn as the spokesperson.

"It's time to make this happen," directed Finn.

Sarge nodded his assent. They'd been wandering around this vicinity of the jungle, trying to identify and mark map coordinates. They could follow the local maps, but the treasure map was presenting a bit of a problem. Part of the ink on the sheet was faded, and they couldn't read some of the notations. Plus, the map itself was cracking. They had to handle it with care, so it wouldn't disintegrate between their fingers.

"Let's take the treasure map and narrow the spot down to our three best guesses. Then we can do a preliminary dig at each of those spots to see which is our winner. Are you game, Sarge?"

"Aye!"

The determined explorers carefully studied the treasure map in comparison to the local charts and pinpointed three target areas. They all looked like strong possibilities for locating the treasure.

"This process isn't going to be easy," remarked Sarge.

"We'll work together — it'll be faster that way," countered Finn.

It took them ten days to check out the first two spots, and they came up empty. There was no sign of any artifacts that would signal buried treasure in either location.

After completing the first two preliminary digs, they collapsed with exhaustion.

Sitting around their fire on the tenth night, Finn and Sarge tried to stay upbeat, but their high hopes were fading along with the embers.

"We can't give up! According to the maps, there were only three possible spots to dig, and now we've ruled out two of them. Are you feeling lucky, Sarge?"

"I feel lucky just to be alive, after all we've been through to get here. If this treasure hunt keeps unfolding in our favor, it wouldn't surprise me."

Sarge continued, "I feel like we were meant to be together sitting by this fire in the middle of the jungle tonight. What happens in the next few days is our destiny. We'll land on our feet either way. I'm ready to turn in so we can get an early start. How about you, buddy?"

No answer. Finn was already asleep.

The next morning, they left at the crack of dawn to investigate the third and final spot. It was hotter than usual already. No doubt the day ahead was going to test them in many ways.

When they reached their destination, it was already noon, and the scorching sun was burning relentlessly through the tall jungle trees. They were both already drenched in sweat and feeling hungry and thirsty. After resting and eating a light lunch, they scrutinized the spot and decided to start digging from two separate angles.

Around 4:00 p.m., Sarge was resting under the tallest tree in the area when he noticed the sun's rays reflecting off something in the underbrush, near the spot where Finn was digging.

"Finn, what's that?"

Finn looked at Sarge then he looked in the direction of Sarge's pointed finger. Together they crawled over the damp foliage to investigate.

Finn pulled a piece of a cracked scabbard out of the dirt. They looked at each other in amazement. Just then it began to pour rain. It didn't matter because the excavators were too excited jumping for joy to notice. With rain caked mud all over them, they looked like a couple of clowns with ridiculous ear-to-ear grins. They were one step closer to finding the buried gold treasure!

Around the campfire that evening, their conversation turned to the next phase of the operation.

"We don't want to let on to the natives that we're digging for gold treasure. The artifacts will serve as the perfect cover for now," warned Finn.

"Aye, we can't underestimate the locals. They might try to outsmart us and grab the treasure."

"We're going to split it with them, but we're not going to tell them yet. Follow my lead. I have a plan," announced Finn.

"Of course, Finn has a plan. He never lets us down," thought Sarge.

"We'll go to the village tomorrow, and make our deal with Tanjona."

Finn and Sarge slept soundly, and awoke

refreshed and ready to implement their new plan. They ate breakfast quickly and then grabbed their backpacks for the hike to the village. Luckily, their trek was uneventful, and they arrived there by late morning.

The village leader invited them into his yurt with his council members. Finn and Sarge sat on the floor in the center of the council ring. Finn got right down to business and laid out his plan.

"We found the site for our archeology dig. We're going to need some help from your villagers to unearth the artifacts. In payment, we will bring in the Unstoppable Foundation to transform this and three adjacent villages."

"What do you mean, they will transform our villages?" asked Tanjona.

"What I mean is that your villages will no longer be poor. They'll set up a school for your children, bring in clean water for all the residents, teach you about nutrition, basic health care, and even show you how to create income. Here is their brochure I found in my parents' belongings. It explains everything."

Tanjona said nothing. He glanced at the brochure and passed it to his council members. Finally, he spoke.

"You will get the help you need to finish your archeology dig. For too many years, our villagers have carried the false hope that gold treasure buried centuries ago by voyaging traders would be discovered to take care of our people. What you bring is real hope."

Finn and the village leader shook hands, and the deal was sealed.

As they hiked back to the yurt, Finn shared with Sarge, "The cost of the Unstoppable Foundation program for four villages is $100,000. We'll be able to fund that from our share of the gold treasure."

Finn was feeling confident in his offer to

help the natives. Tanjona was visualizing his legacy -- helping his and three neighboring villages lift themselves out of poverty. Sarge was keeping his mouth shut about the fact that the dig for the artifacts was a pretense for the dig for gold treasure.

The next morning about forty robust villagers showed up at the yurt, ready to go to work. Finn showed them the archeology dig area, and together they roped off the targeted section. By the end of the day, the work detail had an area about half the size of a football field ready for excavation the next morning.

After three weeks of careful and exhaustive digging with the villagers, Finn and Sarge had an early morning meeting.

Finn laid out the facts. "Our cash is running low. We have about one week of rations left before we'll have to send the villagers home. Plus, we need to pay them as promised."

"What if we cut the crew in half to buy us a

week?" Sarge offered.

"Good plan," responded Finn.

Finn told half of the villagers to go home, which prompted a visit from Tanjona wanting to know if Finn would live up to his deal to bring in the Unstoppable Foundation.

"Absolutely!" Finn told him with his usual confidence.

Sarge was beginning to wonder if they'd finally hit rock bottom.

By the middle of their last funded week to excavate, they were no closer to finding the gold treasure than before. The natives had unearthed some valuable artifacts, but there was no sign of the gold treasure.

Sarge was sitting in the shade muttering to himself. He could see Finn crouched down way off in the corner of the dig site by himself. Holding the treasure map in one hand and a shovel in the other hand, Finn stood slowly and mopped his face. Suddenly Sarge saw that look!

There was no question in Sarge's mind that Finn found the buried gold treasure. They needed to keep their cool. He couldn't react, but Finn knew that Sarge read his body language loud and clear.

That night around the campfire, Finn told the natives he was satisfied with the number of artifacts they helped uncover. They could return to their village tomorrow. He asked them to tell Tanjona that he and Sarge would sort and catalog the objects, which were jobs that required their training as archaeologists.

The next day when Finn and Sarge had the dig area to themselves, they began to unearth the buried treasure. They couldn't sleep for three nights. The bounty exceeded their expectations.

The look and feel of the gold treasure were indescribable. There were ten chests filled with bounty from the traders who had buried them in the late 1700's. All the pieces were well-preserved, and each one carried a tale of adventure that Finn and Sarge would never know. Their new stories would begin as of this day.

Finn and Sarge had to keep their cool.

They separated the chests into two group of five each – one half for them and the other half for the villages. They allocated two pieces of gold from their share to cover the $100,000 Finn promised to fund the Unstoppable Foundation program for four communities. Then they carefully hid the remainder of their half of the treasure.

It was time to revisit Tanjona. Finn turned over the two pieces of gold to him and his council members to make good on his promise of payment for the excavation help from the villagers.

While the rest of the group socialized around the campfire, Finn continued to speak to the leader in low tones. They had a lengthy discussion, ending with a firm handshake and formal bows.

Tanjona then called a special council meeting, and Finn and Sarge returned to the yurt for some much-needed sleep.

The next morning, Sarge woke with a jolt.

"Sarge! Give us a hand here!" hollered Finn.

"What now?" growled Sarge.

Sarge stumbled out of the yurt to discover Tanjona and his council members standing nearby. He saw a dozen villagers trying to pick up and carry the five chests of gold. Their booty was more cumbersome than they expected, so Finn and Sarge lent some muscle to help them transport the treasure to their village.

Then Finn had one more important task he had to do alone.

He visited his parents' graveside and let them know their Madagascar mission was complete. It was a bittersweet one-sided conversation. He hoped it gave them some closure.

When Finn returned from his solemn pilgrimage, he and Sarge took their places at the firepit to plan their triumphant return to Cairo.

And it was to be an even more triumphant return than they ever could have imagined!

15

THE TRIUMPHANT RETURN

No one on the superyacht, *Aquatic Explorer,* expected pirates off the Somalian coast to be a threat. But they were.

Three jet-black speed boats waited near the shoreline and then spread out ahead of the superyacht a mile before it arrived at their coordinates. The superyacht swerved, but the ominous looking speed boats blocked their path! Each ship was carrying ten armed Somalian pirates.

The fearless pirates scaled the superyacht sides with ropes, commandeered the bridge, and held the captain and his crew members hostage. All 50 passengers were ordered to assemble in the central dining room with their money and jewelry.

With menacing eyes, the pirates stripped the terrified passengers of their cash. Then the threatening pirates forced the captain to open the ship's safe from which they grabbed piles of currency.

The pirates estimated their take in cash to be about six million dollars. They imagined their peers hailing them as the Somalians who pulled off the first ever successful pirate attack of a superyacht in the Gulf of Aden!

Three of the pirates were dispatched to stash all the stolen cash in their speedboats. They followed orders to divide it among the three boats.

After robbing the captain, crew, and passengers of all their cash, the greedy pirates then collected all the precious jewels from the wealthy people on board the superyacht. What a heist!

Once the pirates stashed the stolen jewels in their three boats, they regrouped on the *Aquatic Explorer*, awaiting orders from their pirate leader.

No one could have predicted what happened next. Simultaneously, the Captain and the pirate leader gazed at the horizon in disbelief.

They saw a small yacht piloted by a young boy and a middle-aged man towing three black speedboats by steel cables. The pair's nimble vessel was cruising at almost 60 mph, leaving the 30 pirates trapped with the Captain, his crew, and 50 angry and resourceful passengers.

What the Captain and the pirate leader didn't see was the passengers and crew members sending silent signals to each other to reposition themselves to overtake the pirates and seize their weapons.

In a flash, the passengers and crew put an end to the bungled siege. They locked the pirates below deck until the authorities took them into custody.

The pirates were scorned and jailed for launching the most incompetent pirate attack of a superyacht in the Gulf of Aden!

EPILOG

On the fourth largest island in the world, Madagascar, the residents of more than fifty villages are enjoying vastly improved living conditions. They now have clean water, health care, and schools. The spokesperson for the region's turnaround, Tanjona, a humble leader of a small village, promises there will be more and more transformed villages in Madagascar and neighboring communities in Eastern Africa. The source of their apparently unlimited funding is unknown, but the project seems to be unstoppable.

In Cairo, the City of a Thousand Minarets, Sarge and Finn enjoy starting their days of leisure with the sunrise about 5:00 a.m. They usually greet each other on their adjacent balconies, which span the rooftops of their two luxurious mansions in the Garden City district of Central Cairo. They both enjoy living in an upscale and secure neighborhood. They don't have to worry about street thieves!

On this June morning, the citizens of Cairo awake to some good news and some bad news. The good news is that contractors found the long-lost artifacts and art objects from an unsolved crime in a Cairo slum, buried at the site of new construction.

The bad news is that the authorities took into custody one of Cairo's famous and decorated Police Detectives, Amanda Strong, a.k.a. Simone Spivey, for her alleged role in the theft and burial of the stolen goods. The police aren't disclosing the source of the tip, other than to say it is credible, having come from a known criminal informant in El Salvador.

With restrained delight and bemused

expressions, Sarge and Finn devour the morning news and then raise their breakfast champagne glasses in a rooftop toast to the power of karma. They are proud they traveled the high road and saw justice served.

ABOUT THE AUTHORS

Seamus Tracy

Seamus Tracy, Marge Brown's 12-year-old grandson, is an author of books and video game reviews. He currently resides in Michigan and has lived in Maine, Connecticut, and Virginia. He lives with his sisters, parents, turtle, and dog. He loves to write and play games such as Dungeons and Dragons and Warhammer 40k.

Marge Brown

Marge Brown, Seamus Tracy's maternal grandmother, is an author and digital publisher. She is married to Bruce Brown, a freelance journalist. They reside in Leland, North Carolina with their dog, Happy. They visit their children and grandchildren in Kentucky, Michigan, and California as much as possible.

Made in the USA
Middletown, DE
20 November 2018